The station is very busy.
Mummy holds my hand very tightly,
and I hold on to Teddy's hand tightly too.

We're taking a train to Grandpa's house.
The train makes lots of stops.
Some people get off, and then
even more people get on.
I wonder where everyone is going.

Suddenly Mummy says,
"This is our stop!"

We rush off the train. The doors slam shut behind us.
We're standing on the platform when I realise
I don't have Teddy.

The whistle blows. Mummy and I watch
as the train leaves the station with Teddy still on it.

"Don't worry," says Mummy.
"We'll get Teddy back."

At Grandpa's house I feel very sad without Teddy.
Grandpa finds one of Mummy's old toy bears for me to cuddle,
but it's not the same.

That night when I fall asleep I dream about Teddy.
In my dream, he takes me to a special place.
It's a sort of magical room where all the lost things go.
It is full of all kinds of things that people
have forgotten or left behind.

Inside, I find all the things I have ever lost.

There is my favourite orange jacket, which I left on the bus.

A giant beach ball that floated out to sea.

A special purple hair clip.

My superhero lunchbox.

A long overdue library book.

One stripy sock, one spotty sock
and one long flowery sock.

And Teddy.

In the morning, I tell Grandpa all about my dream.
"You've given me an idea," he says.
"I think I know where we might find your Teddy."

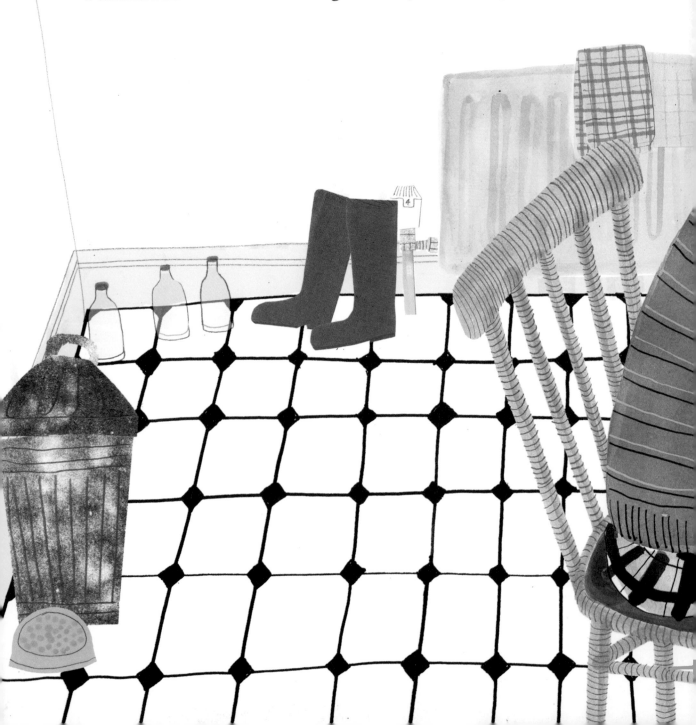

Grandpa and I take the train back to the busy station.
Grandpa holds my hand very tightly,
and I hold on tightly too.

We walk out of the station,
down the road and round the corner.
"Ah! Here it is!" says Grandpa.
I look up and read the sign above the door:
Lost Property Office.

LOST

LOST CAT

Inside, Grandpa and I join a queue of people
who have also lost things.
A man has lost his umbrella,
a lady has lost her keys
and a little boy has lost his bike.
Finally, Grandpa and I get to the desk.
"I've lost my teddy" I say.
"A teddy bear? Well we have
a lot of those," says the lady.
"You'd better come with me."

I follow her down a long corridor,
and into a room. The room is filled with
shelves, from the floor all the way up to
the ceiling. On each shelf there is
row upon row of lost things.

Just like in my dream.

We go past all the umbrellas, all the glasses,
all the hats and all the keys.

Past all the bags, and balls, and rows of books. Past a violin, a clown puppet, a toy dinosaur, some false teeth, a hosepipe, a sparkly party dress, a bird mask . . . and all sorts of strange and wonderful objects.

Each one belonging to somebody.
Each one left behind somewhere.

Finally, we get to the shelf
full of teddy bears.
There are big yellow ones,
small pink ones,
old ones, new ones,
fluffy ones and ugly ones.
And then, high up on a shelf,

I see Teddy.

The lady reaches up
and hands Teddy to me.
I give Teddy a big hug
and say
"Thank you"
to the lady.

We go back through the busy station.
I hold Grandpa's hand very tightly,
and I hold on to Teddy tightly too.
All the way home.

For F.N. and H.F.

First published 2018
This edition published 2020 by order of the Tate Trustees by Tate Publishing,
a division of Tate Enterprises Ltd, Millbank, London SW1P 4RG
www.tate.org.uk/publishing

Text and illustrations © Emily Rand 2020

A catalogue record for this book is available from the British Library

ISBN 978 1 84976 732 3

Distributed in the United States and Canada by ABRAMS, New York
Library of Congress Control Number applied for

Colour reproduction by Evergreen Colour Management Ltd
Printed in China by Toppan Leefung Printing Ltd

MIX
Paper from responsible sources
FSC® C104723

Here are some other books to enjoy from Emily Rand and Tate Publishing: